W0081903

my MOM

words & pictures

For my mom, Millie—SQ
For D, J and S—SM

© 2025 Quarto Publishing Group USA Inc.
Text © 2025 Susan Quinn
Illustrations © 2025 Sarah Mathew

Susan Quinn has asserted her right to be identified
as the author of this work.

Sarah Mathew has asserted her right to be identified
as the illustrator of this work.

Editor: Alice Hobbs
Senior Designer: Sarah Chapman-Suire
Creative Director: Malena Stojić
Associate Publisher: Holly Willsher
Production Manager: Nikki Ingram

First published in 2025 by words & pictures,
an imprint of The Quarto Group.
100 Cummings Center,
Suite 265D Beverly,
MA 01915, USA.
T (978) 282-9590 F (978) 283-2742
www.quarto.com

No part of this publication may be reproduced, stored in a retrieval system,
or transmitted in any form or by any means, electronic, mechanical, photocopying,
recording, or otherwise, without the prior permission of the publisher, nor be
otherwise circulated in any form of binding or cover other than that in which
it is published and without a similar condition being
imposed on the subsequent purchaser.
All rights reserved.

A CIP record for this book is available from the Library of Congress.

ISBN: 978-0-7112-9669-5

Manufactured in Guangdong, China
TT112024
9 8 7 6 5 4 3 2 1

MIX
Paper | Supporting
responsible forestry
FSC® C016973
FSC
www.fsc.org

SUSAN QUINN   SARAH MATHEW

my
MOM

words&pictures

My mom says that
when I arrived

I was like
a star

drifting

down

from the sky

and into
her life.

It was the day she had dreamed about—but thought may never happen. The day that we started

OUR AMAZING ADVENTURE,

TOGETHER...

Every day Mom thinks of places
to go and games for us to play.

We sail a ship
around the garden.

We take a rocket into space
and have picnics on the Moon.

If I break one of my toys or Teddy
has an accident, it makes me sad.

But Mom says she will
fix it—and she does, because
Mom can fix anything!

Sometimes, when we go to the park
I get scared meeting new friends.

But when Mom is by my side,
I feel safe and strong.

When it's sunny
we go exploring.

We hop across streams
on stepping stones.

We run though a meadow of wildflowers and make lots of daisy chains.

We stomp through
deep, dark woods.
We run as fast as
the wind.

Then we climb up,
up, up
the big hill . . .

Up
to the top
of the world!

We build castles
made of golden sand.

We go jumping in the waves.

We look for shells in rock pools
and make seaweed garlands
to wear like crowns.

When it's cold and raining we paint pictures. We dance and we jump and we sing!

We build a den that's cozy and
warm, where Mom makes up
stories to make me laugh.

If there's snow on the ground,
we wear warm coats and boots.
We put food out for the birds to eat.
Then we build a big snow bear!

When I'm cross because I can't find Teddy, Mom helps me to look for him in the jungle.

And when we find him —
Mom gives us **both**
a great **big** hug!

Mom reads to me at bedtime,
as we snuggle up tight.
And when I start to yawn . . .
Mom cuddles me until I fall asleep.

And when I sleep,
I dream of Mom
and all the adventures
that we have.

But sometimes,
if I can't sleep . . .

Mom tells me how she
loved me when I was just
a dream. And when I see
my mom so happy—
I'm really, really glad
she dreamed of me!